One Night With A Vampire

Clair Gardenwell

Published by Clair Gardenwell, 2021.

This is a work of fiction. Similarities to real people, places, or events are entirely coincidental.

ONE NIGHT WITH A VAMPIRE

First edition. November 8, 2021.

Copyright © 2021 Clair Gardenwell.

ISBN: 979-8201681449

Written by Clair Gardenwell.

Also by Clair Gardenwell

Alexandra Van Helsing
Bite Me

Sisters of the Fae
FoxFire
Owl's Flight

Stand With Me
Foxgloves Are For Deception

The Scarlet Huntress
Dawn

Standalone

Tell Me No Lies
One Night With A Vampire
Swept Away

Table of Contents

1

"Thank you so much! Please come again!" My hand flicked in a jaunty wave towards the departing backside of my last customer of the evening. Vanishing into the night streets with the cheery tinkle of the little bell strand attached to the door as music, I let out a long sigh, scrubbing my hand across my bleary grey eyes to try and get rid of a little bit of the tension starting to throb in my temples. It sure had been a long day, the kind of long empty day where the customers barely trickled in, and we had more food left over than we had served all day. I know the pandemic sickness had played a big turn in keeping people away from crowding in restaurants, but since the big Vitamin D discovery had almost kicked it in the pants, I was hoping things would get better.

I was wrong.

If I had a handful of customers all day, it was a small miracle, and my cafe was slowly sinking into the red as the bills piled higher. If something didn't change soon, everything my family had worked so hard for would be just like some of the other buildings on Main Street. The windows boarded up and the doors locked tight forever.

"Yo, Darc-master! Do you want these Pumpkin Delight Pies loaded up for the shelter? There's four we didn't break into today." Sticking his strawberry blonde head through the small pickup window separating the kitchen from the service counter, Josh's reddish sable and deep cobalt eyes sparkled with good humor. A flash of a slightly crooked laughing smile showed brilliant white teeth against the background of his crisp sun kissed tan, the human version of a Golden Retriever if there ever was one. Josh, my cook, one of my best friends since 2nd grade, and the world's most unlikely to succeed in magic warlock leaned one leanly muscled arm against the window, and twitched a thick reddish brow up. "We've also got lots of ingredients left for the Chicken Parmesan rolls left, both the clucking version and the veggie version. You want me to whip up a batch to go?"

I sighed, letting the back of my head flop against the cool kiss of the glass. I was so hoping that our special menu of Josh's Chicken Parmesan sandwich rolls might tempt a few customers on this brisk autumn day. With their perfectly puffed golden crust, rich marinara sauce seasoned with his own special blend of herbs, long ropes of creamy mozzarella, and hearty chunks of meat or imitation meat. It was all topped off by the Pumpkin Delight Pies that were my own special creation. A creamy pumpkin pudding base in a cinnamon graham crust, and topped with a cloud of the lightest whipped cream you'll ever taste. The two formed a beautiful combination together, but sadly the doors opened so little that the dead autumn leaves that blew down the street had decided to take a nap outside my door. "Yeah, sure. Someone might as well enjoy them."

"Oh, but think of all the good work you're doing! I'm sure that your aura must be brighter than ever!" Meadow trilled like a small songbird, only interrupted by the scratch of the broom bristles against the smooth black and white checkerboard tile floor. Her long rainbow braids hung down to her waist, swaying in time with the loose fabric of her white peasant blouse as she swept the random bits of trash up into a small dustpan.

I'm more than happy to do it, but I do have to pay the bills. So, it would be nice to have just a little more business to help with things." Pushing off the door, I walked over and knelt down. Taking the dustpan and holding it at a slight angle so she could sweep the small pile of trash in it, I glanced up and saw that her dark almond shaped eyes had taken on a more serious glaze.

Her strokes slowed, the broom coming to rest against the well-worn leather sandal on her left foot. Pulled over by the weight of her braids or maybe she was just lost in that much deep thought, her head tilted to the side and her gaze traveled up to the ceiling. "Of course, you know I tell everyone in my classes about how great the food is here, but maybe I could try hanging a few posters around the campus. I don't think it would work as well as direct word of mouth, but it's worth a try." With a definitive nod that her entire willow thin body bobbing along with her, I could see the brilliant mind that lurked underneath the 60's hippie style clothes was churning just as fast as it could.

"Thanks, I'd appreciate it." I said just as sincerely as I could, taking the dustpan in one hand and straightening up, my hand briefly patted her shoulder and it was like someone turned on the sun. Meadow started beaming, the entire room lighting up just from her smile, and she bounced off to take the dustpan out of my hand and empty it in the kitchen trash.

"Have you thought about the catering business anymore? I know that your first attempt yesterday turned out to be a massive crap load, but you could try again?" A second, deeper voice startled me slightly, and I turned to see one of my other MVP employees easily tilting the chairs up on the table with one hand. Axe didn't smile so much as glare thoughtfully, the simple black t-shirt stretched tight across his rock-hard biceps and chest, and my heart started to pound fast as those wild golden eyes locked tight on mine. An army buddy of Josh's, I wasn't sure about hiring the half feral werewolf at first glance, but he had quickly turned into quite the dependable employee. As long as there were no screaming kids, super demanding crush of customers, and obnoxious vampires.

"I don't actually know. Since that Chocolate Cherry Blood Cake that I spent several hours on is still sitting in my cooler, there's no hope of at least getting a partial refund as both sides of the wedding party are now dust in the wind. But I probably will." I sighed again, my gaze roaming up the pale mint walls to where Grandma and Grandpa's picture hung just over the register. Taken in black and white, but still smiling with their arms wrapped around each other's shoulders. This place was a Crescent City icon for good food and happiness, and I couldn't let it die. No matter how many times the outdated kitchen wiring blew a fuse, the drippy faucet in the ladies' bathroom ran up the utility bill, and more scars of age decided to crack open further. I had three generations of Name Your Slice Blanchard's riding on my shoulders, and I refused to let me, Darcy Blanchard, be the one that let it die.

"Darcy! You won't believe it!" Higher pitched than a hawk scream and almost as annoyingly loud. Renea, my business partner, tumbled into the dining room through the swinging kitchen doors, and just barely avoided falling flat on her face. Like a sparkly faerie dressed in bubblegum pink, the cheery drop waist dress skimmed just above her knees, the floaty layers of fabric a sharp contrast to the stiffness of the white plaster cast that encased her left leg from toe to mid-calf, and the classy brunette bob. We just got a call from Count von Dracula's assistant. Their special dessert caterer went kerplunk, something about an engine overheating, and they want you to bring in some of your fabulous Chocolate Blood-Cherry cake for his 1200th birthday party! Isn't that great?" The clunk-clunk of her metal crutches just barely skated on this side of sturdy, almost spearing Axe right in the foot, and she tilted dangerously on the border of falling backwards with each step.

"Watch it, Glitterbomb!" He snarled, pointed white canines flashing behind curled lips. Axe tossed his head, the sharp plains of his high cheekbones growing even sharper as the wolf muzzle threatened to rip forward. My breath hitched, my legs already burning with the urge to run in case he went full wolf, but he didn't. Instead, he closed his eyes. His broad shoulders heaved with a heavy forced breath, a flush darkening the deep bronze of his skin, and he ripped a hand through the shock of his shoulder length raven dark hair before stomping off through the kitchen. Tossing a few curses in his mother's native Cherokee over his shoulder for good measure.

"Gee, what's his problem?" Renea wondered out loud, her train of thought distracted for the moment.

"Considering that you almost smashed his foot with your crutch, and it's a full moon tonight, I think that should explain it all. But what I want to know is why you ran in here screaming like a banshee about Count von Dracula, and how on earth you could expect me to cater some party on short notice. *Really* short notice in less than... how long is it?"

Her pale bony shoulders lifted up in a shrug. "About three hours. That's more than enough time since you've already got the cake sitting in the cooler. All you have to do is just scrape off the word marriage and change it to birthday. The Count doesn't really want people seeing his full age more than possible, and Josh can throw together a few more nibbles for the party guests. You do know how fast the word will travel about this place on that line, right? The Von Dracula's are Crescent City's most influential family, and we'll do so much business that it will be rolling out our ears. What's the big deal?"

"The big deal is that I can't serve a cake I already made for another customer to Count von Dracula! And even if I did, it might not be enough. Did you even ask if they needed a 3-, 4-, or 5-layer cake depending on how many people they have attending? That alone could take several hours to assemble since I have to make sure the blood-cherry liquor ratio is just right. Plus, the dark chocolate frosting, and then there is the travel time. How on earth could you agree to something like that?" I knew the answer to that question already. She was seeing dollar signs, and when Renea Sutherland smelled money, there wasn't any stopping her. If it wasn't for Renea's generous funds from her family's extensive mattress selling fortune, my cafe would never have limped along as long as it has.

She smiled, the matching pink lipstick adding a deceptively innocent mask to the devilish grin her features were currently bearing. "Oh, please. I've seen worse. It's perfectly fine. What's the worst that could happen?"

Famous last words.

2

"What could go wrong is that I could lose my license if the Health Board finds out I'm serving leftover items to my customers." I slid my hand back through my hair, the tangled mass of curly red strands tugging painfully at the messy bun I had shoved it in earlier. "Plus, I can't serve that to the most important vampire in town! It's a day old, and I have it earmarked for the homeless shelter down the street!" Floundering like a fish, I could feel that I was losing this battle altogether.

"Honey, with the money we stand to make from this event alone. You can buy enough supplies to keep the shelter going for the rest of the year. Plus," She paused, clunking forward a half step and throwing a sassy wink my way. "There's always the possibility that you could snag a rich vampire's eye."

I blinked, so stunned that if she slapped me, I still wouldn't be able to speak. Me? My current taste in men apparently leads to the completely unreliable and steals your cat's medicine to sell on the street type. Even when I tried, that didn't include super sexy and completely mysterious vampires. Even super rich ones like the Count von Dracula family who were so secretive that only a few people actually knew what he looked like. The most prominent one was the count himself, a grandfatherly gentleman with white hair and thick black caterpillar brows who was always photographed in a perfectly pressed suit. Hell, I had a better chance of going out in the woods with a box of dental floss and catching Bigfoot. I shook my head. "I don't know what kind of pain medication that they have you on, but you're pretty delusional if you think that I have a chance at even floating in their same circle as the super-rich. Plus, I'm horrible at parties. You know that. Why don't we send Josh?"

"I second that!" An eager hand flew out the service window followed by his grinning face, Josh's long body trying to stuff itself through the small space and out the other side. Axe pulled him back before his shoulders could ever clear, the two landing with a hard thump on the kitchen floor. My jaw slipped a little slack when something popped and started smoking, mixing with the deep throated snarls and Meadow's surprised squeaks. I wonder if my insurance covers damage by warlock and werewolf?

She shook her head, the ends of her bob swaying to and fro against her chin. "No way in hell! As soon as he stepped foot on the place and saw a pretty face, then he'd be off for the rest of the night."

"What about Axe?"

"Really? You're going to send the half feral, half deaf werewolf to represent your business, *and* into a vampire's home? That's a recipe for disaster if I ever saw one."

A pool of sticky sweat started to gather around my neck, slinking like a tiny river down my spine, and I flapped one hand against my chest for a little breeze. "What about Meadow?"

"Oh, grow a steel vagina!" Slamming the tip of one crutch against the floor, my attention snapped back to Renea as her glare threw silent daggers straight at my heart. "If I was out of this boot, I'd be out there in a minute working my way through the party just to have a chance at breathing with the movers and shakers of this town. If you have to, look at it like this. You love Name Your Slice, right?"

"That goes without saying." I nodded, narrowing my eyes slightly. What was she up to?

"This is your typical everyday business transaction. Number one, you are providing Count von Dracula with a line of service that no one else can even touch. Your special dessert recipes like the cake are something that no one else in Crescent City touches, right? All those recipes that you and your grandma concocted are the reason that I'm not a size 2 anymore." She laughed, shaking her non-existent rear for added measure. "But you would bet your bunions that if Count von Dracula said jump, I'd say where and how high."

"That's just it! You don't get it!" A disgusted sigh crept out before I could stop it. "I don't want to keep my business because I mooched off some high and mighty person! That's not how I was raised. You work hard, stay true, and do what you love. That's the secret." Alright, now I'm just over it. I started to walk behind the counter, but she held out one crutch and blocked my way. "Move it, Renea! I'm tired, filthy, and sore. I'm not in the mood to play games." My lips curled up in a snarl worthy of Axe himself.

"You might be, but you're also going to pack up and go partying with the richest crowd in town." She smelled victory; I could see it in her eyes. That glow of confidence that made her pointed chin stubbornly stick out, and her bony little neck look like something that might belong to a turkey. One by one, my walls started to crumble with exhaustion, each brick slowly collapsing into dust.

"I can't dance," I warned her, not that she didn't know that since she was wearing the very visible results of the one waltzing class she pushed us in. I didn't mean to let go of my partner's arm when he guided me into a spin, and I swear I didn't mean to push her right into the punchbowl table. "And I don't have anything to wear."

"It's fine, I've got stuff to get you through. This is high society; you'll be lucky to see someone that isn't so ancient that they fart out dust. Don't forget about the gossip section either, they'll be watching your every move." Hobbling along on the heel of her boot, she looped one arm through mine and steered me right back towards the kitchen. Still chattering the whole way. "I'm feeling a little Cinderella moment going on here. Why don't we go and see if we can't conjure up a new outfit for you that's fairy tale perfect? You'll be the real belle of the ball!"

"Don't worry, Darcy." Popping up in the window like a wild daisy, Meadow's beaming smile couldn't even soothe away the butterflies that were popping up in my stomach. No, scratch that. Make that vultures that were flying around. Great big vultures of impending doom instead of cute little butterflies of dread. "You'll be perfectly fine."

Flopping on top of her head with the sleeve of his chef whites rolled up to his elbows, I could see the talons of the screaming eagle that was inked into Josh's left bicep. "Yeah, you'll be great, Darcy." His smile was warm and soft, like caramel pudding fresh off the stove. Maybe it was plum pudding based on the purple ring that was starting to swell his left eye. "There's no doubt that you have all the money bags eating right out of the palm of your hand."

A third head drifted into view, one that wasn't so much smiling but nodding in encouragement. "Just remember the goal of your mission, and don't let any obstacles stand in your way." That was it for Axe's encouragement. He blinked slowly, a ghost of a smirk twisting one side of his lips up. "And a formal event with liquor is the perfect time to gather any unsightly bits of information that some people would do anything to hide."

With three smiling faces and one somber one encouraging me on, something close to a sickly smile pasted itself on my lips, but I couldn't really feel it because my face was numb. Have I mentioned before that I hate parties? As in despise the very idea until the dark squishy guts pop out the back kind of hatred?

This was going to be horrible. I just know it.

3

First things first. Vampires revealed themselves to the general public about 20 years ago, and they were *everywhere*. Starting from your local garbageman to the typical rich billionaire like pops up in all the romance novels, the fear that ran rampant when they first came out had just faded away. Now nobody would give a second glance if they saw a couple feeding off one another in broad daylight, or if someone ordered a cup of blood infused coffee instead of a regular cappuccino. I, personally, found them to be wonderful, if very fussy customers. Plus, the typically deep pockets that ran from so many years of living could make a nice bump in my personal finances as long as the service was just perfect.

But that's for your normal, everyday vampires. Not the Von Dracula family.

Count Von Dracula and his four children were the oldest, most well-respected vampire family in Crescent City. Probably the most powerful too if the rumors were true that he was *the* Count Dracula, but it had never been publicly confirmed by any member of the family. I didn't know a lot myself, just that they were quite skilled in business, the type of rich that was a hit with the old money crowd, and so secretive that not even the gossip rag reporters could get past the foreboding black iron gates. They also spared quite a bit of their considerable fortune with the town, helping fund the local natural history museum, a hospital wing for dementia patients, and the animal shelter. Making them a big favorite with the mayor, but they never attended the fundraising events publicly. That's why this party was such a big deal, not only was it the Count's birthday, but it was a chance to enter into the mysterious world of the Von Dracula's for one night.

And me, little ole me, had a private pass right past the swirled V and D embedded in the thick iron gate, and right to the service entrance of the sprawling mansion.

My six-inch heels clicked loudly against the elaborately polished red oak floors, the thin black velvet straps barely holding onto my ankles as I click-clacked my way towards the ballroom. With my generous curves stuffed into the drapey A-line violet evening gown Renea had produced, the elegant floor length chiffon fabric was cinched just under my breasts. The delicate pleats gave the illusion of me actually having a defined waist, just as long as I didn't breathe too much. The deep plunging v neck, in both the front and the back, would probably give a few more conservative vampires a stroke at seeing so much of my neck. The long sheer sleeves were more shawl than sleeve as they reached down almost to the floor, draping into the filmy fabric of the skirt. A few added touches of makeup to disguise the freckles across my nose, some kind of fruity smelling hairspray, and my unruly curls had been tamed beyond belief. Formed into a thick Dutch braid running partway down the backside of my head, with the ending strands dangling thick between my shoulders.

I was beautiful. I was elegant. I was totally out of my mind.

I stood in a narrow hallway, the grand ballroom looming ahead like a monster's cave straight out of a horror movie. Packed cheek to jowl with fancy people in long glittering gowns of every jewel color imaginable, and dark tuxes with cute bow ties and long tails. I saw the chubby figure of the mayor with his smooth head gleaming in the soft light, and Mrs. Tisdale from the library was beautiful in her pearl encrusted evening gown. I don't know where she found it, but her barely five-foot frame was perfectly captured, not dragging the floor in the least. A couple swirled by in a blur of fabric, Mr. and Mrs. Patel dancing an elegant waltz as the rumbling buzz of pleasant conversation clawed my ears like a screeching fire alarm. Completely overriding the calming classical music floating through the air from the six-string quartet, my gaze flicked over so many faces I knew, and my legs seized up.

Blind panic puffed up in my veins like a freshly done waffle, and it sent me diving behind a conveniently placed potted palm further down the hall. Renea was out of her mind to think that I could do this. Business inquiries I could handle, but not an elegant party. Just blindly stepping up and starting a conversation with a stranger? It's a nightmare. My throat was already starting to close up, and I haven't even talked to anyone yet!

A small, almost noiseless, squeak from behind made me glance over my shoulder, and I heaved a sigh of relief as a slender waiter popped out of a small door at the end of the hall. The elegant round silver tray perched on one hand looked like it would collapse any minute from all the sparkling champagne flutes, but somehow it didn't. The fizzy golden liquid matched the peach trimmed walls perfectly, and I was so thirsty that I could have drained the whole tray if I tried.

"Hey!" I croaked, reaching out and snagging his elbow before he could pass by.

"Madam, please." The waiter shot a glance down the slope of his long nose. The haughty upper crust English accent somehow made the words sound like they were about to slap me with a pair of flawless white gloves. "If you are searching for the washroom, it is just down the hall. Our greenery is NOT an acceptable alternative no matter how urgent your needs are."

Crap! Could this get any more embarrassing?

"I'm not searching for the bathroom!" I hissed, my cheeks flaming worse than a grill right now. "I'm the replacement supplier of the dessert for the event, and I need to find whoever is in charge of the food so that I can get my check." And possibly try to salvage some sort of reputation out of this place.

"Oh, *that*." Waiter boy rolled his eyes so far up in his head that they should have gotten stuck. He shifted his tray from his left hand to his right, flicking a dismissive finger towards the door he had entered from. "Our event coordinator, Monsieur Jacques Fontebleu, is currently supervising the kitchen and he will make sure that your name is on the list to be paid for your services. If you wish to speak with him, he will be the small man in the distasteful bubblegum pink shirt. Now, if you will excuse me. I have duties to attend to."

Effectively cutting off any further attempt at conversation, the Waiter shifted the loaded tray back to his left hand, tucked his right behind his back, and sauntered his way out into the crushing crowd with his nose still perched high. I was so stunned that I didn't even make a squeak, but my fingers still twitched with the urge to tie the dangling ends of his suit jacket tails into a knot just to see what he might do.

My head whipped back and forth, quickly making sure that no one else was looking before I darted towards the door like an escaped convict seeking freedom. But it wasn't the freedom I was searching for. My body smacked face first into something hard and cool, two hands quickly fluttering to my shoulders, and latched on with a grip so tight that I could feel it in my bones. My hands instinctively drew up to my chest, my lips rounded up into a little O of shock, and I found myself face to face with a set of vampire black eyes. "Watch yourself, darling. This isn't a good place to be idly wandering around." The voice drawled like a lazy river, sweet and slow as it wrapped around my ears like a cozy blanket. My eyes were glued to the set of plump lips hovering right at eye level, the very same ones that were marked by a small trickle of crimson at the corner.

"I-Um, W-was looking for the kitchen!" My tongue finally floundered out, giving my head a quick shake to clear it, I blinked sharply and forced my eyes up and away. Holy shit, he was gorgeous. With flawless olive toned skin, thick dark hair that fell around his face in luscious waves, and the type of lips that could conjure up the most sinful of fantasies. The vampire chuckled softly under his breath, one slightly warm hand cupping around my left palm, and his long fingers gracefully folded through mine.

"Well, we can't have a beautiful lady such as this out wandering about all by herself." His teeth flash bright, showing off the full length of those impressive canines. A slip of scarlet muscle slides between them, gliding along the length of his full lower lip like a phantom. My heart pounds, shaking my ribs like someone doing the Irish Stepdance. I'm sure he could hear it, the predatory smile splitting his face grows in size, and a river of icy fear courses down my spine. Crap, crap, crap! I need to get out of here!"

"Uh, no thanks! I know just where I need to be! See ya!" Anywhere away from here is the answer to that. Before he could move, I slung his hand away and dashed for the kitchen door. It opened easily with a little push, and suddenly I was thrown from the fiery attention of a vampire into a sea of pure chaos. A many armed mass of chef's whites and frantically moving arms shifted from stainless steel table to steel table. Sharp knives flashed in a seamless silver blur, mercilessly chopping whatever crisp yellow and green vegetables passed by into tiny minced slices. Round white stoneware plates were passed back and forth between grabbing hands, each set depositing either a lump of browned meat or the ruby wriggling mass of a blood pudding. The elegant black suited waiters hovered like phantoms, whisking away a finished plate just as soon as a cook released it. It was a beautiful dance actually. A very skilled one because if someone made a single mistake, it would all be broken.

"Excuse me!" One of the waiters rushed by with his tray loaded full of crisp salads, the silver edge breezed by my head so close that I could see every swirl of the ornate carvings around the rim. I yelped, staggering back three steps until my butt collided with the cool tile covered wall.

"The waitstaff is in a pretty big rush, so it kinda helps to just stay over here out of the way." A soft voice chuckled lightly, the warm rasp of his light accent hugging each word like a lover's caress, and I turned to see a slender guy sitting crossed legged on top of the counter next to me. A huge carton of ice cream balanced between the v of his legs, his soft honey-colored eyes blinked at me curiously, one slender hand holding out a silver spoonful of creamy vanilla ice cream speckled with dark flecks of chocolate chips. "Wanna bite?"

4

Um… what? My eyes flashed up and down, taking in every inch of the silky black tuxedo that pooled around his bent knees, his shoulders hiked up with sharp creases like someone had pulled a puppet string along his back. His matching black bowtie was tilted down to the left, one flap of his pearly white dress shirt draped out over his waist, and his dark waistcoat was stained with more than a few blobs of melted ice cream and a couple reddish splotches as well. The neck and head of a sapphire blue dragon playfully curled up and over along the left side of his throat, like it couldn't wait to play peek-a-boo, and his faux hawk was rocking a matching hue frosting on the longer tips of his ebony dark hair. A quirky smile wavered at one corner of his full lips, but it threatened to break like glass at any moment. He looked almost as nervous as I felt.

"Where did you come from? I know that you weren't sitting there a moment ago!" I blurted out, but then immediately regretted it. Maybe the encounter with Mr. Creepy Vampire had left me too uneasy. Every trace of the warm olive tone in his skin drained away like someone had pulled the plug, his round cheeks paled like he had just been converted to a ghost, and the spoon slipped out of his fingers. Landing in the tub of ice cream with a wet thud, his limp hand was still hanging in midair and his fingers twitched awkwardly like half dead worms. Crap! I didn't mean to break him.

"Um… I've been sitting here the whole time. But it's no big deal. I'm a pretty easy guy to miss." With that said, he dropped his head and seemed to refocus on the carton of ice cream sitting between his legs. Quickly rounding up the spoon and popping it straight into his mouth, I held my gaze a moment longer because something was starting to nag at me. Like I knew him from somewhere, but I couldn't place it. Maybe it was just me, knowing how it feels being the socially awkward rat in a party, but it seemed like he had a lot of trouble hiding behind those words. Renae had said that I needed to talk to people to help bump up business, and this guy felt like he could use a friendly ear right about now.

I hiked my long skirt up in my fists, the silky fabric of my sleeves pulling back to show off the old wrinkled burn scars from hot batter splatters curling around my forearms, and hopped up on the counter beside him. "Is everything okay?" I tilted my head to the side, trying to get a better look at his face, and the end of my braid scraped against my neck. "I know usually when I dive into a thing of ice cream like that, it's usually because I'm going through a bad break up." His gaze shyly flicked over to me, but retreated back to his ice cream just as quick like it was his safe spot. "I don't mind listening if you need to vent."

The spoon twirled around between his forefinger and thumb, his shoulders slumping so badly that it looked like his entire body was trying to fold in on himself. "It shouldn't really matter." He finally whispered, and I had to lean forward just to hear him over the clanking clatter from the kitchen staff. "I'm used to getting stood up a lot, almost every single date, but tonight was really important. It's my dad's birthday party, and my sister set me up with someone she knew, and... the lady took one look at me and started fake gagging like she was having an asthma attack or something. Now my sister will be pissed because she'll think it was my fault that I scared her off." He chuckled bitterly, cramming another spoonful of ice cream into his mouth, and closed his eyes with a little blissed out moan. "Oh, god. This is the best stuff ever!"

Damn! Poor guy. He sounded like he had my kind of luck in the relationship world. "I'm sure that your sister will understand. It wasn't your fault. I was called in at the last minute to cater the dessert for this event, and my business partner is just convinced that if I oozed around the party, I might drum up a little business for my cafe. That's a lot of pressure for someone who was clinging to one of those potted palm trees like it could save her life. I really need to gain the support of someone in the Von Dracula family, but I'm hiding in the kitchen too." Reaching down beside my thighs, my hand found the handle of a drawer, and quickly latched on. It popped out to reveal one of the utensils storage systems, and I quickly snagged a spoon out and dipped it into the ice cream. It was very firm, but still slightly soft. Peeling up into my spoon in an even curl of creamy white. He was absolutely right; it was totally delicious! The thick creamy sweetness flooded my mouth with hints of toasted vanilla, the crunchy chocolate chips not quite as sweet due to a hint of pleasant bitterness, and both of them melted together to form heaven living right on my tongue.

A few choked gasps broke me right out of my haze, and that's when I realized that a little lingering moan was creeping out of my throat, and it wasn't cute like his. This was the type of moan that I always tried to keep private. Why did I have to keep embarrassing myself around strangers? My eyes snapped open wide, my heart kicking up into a rib bruising speed, and the spoon dropped from my hands. "Um..." He coughed lightly into his fist, ignoring the clatter of the spoon hitting the floor, and his voice was a touch raspier than before. A small movement down below drew my eyes down, his hand restlessly smoothing over the wrinkled fabric of one thigh. When my gaze pulled back up, I sucked in a sharp breath through my teeth. Fat streaks of deep ruby had stained the honey of his wide stretched eyes, the tips of two pearly white fangs appearing in the slight gap of his parted lips.

Oh, he's a vampire just like the other one. That's... interesting. I didn't think they liked ice cream that much if it didn't have blood mixed in.

Twisting one side of his lips up into an awkward smile, his legs started to jiggle like he couldn't be still a moment longer. "You obviously have never met my sister. She's a hurricane on a good day, and has apparently decided that I have to grow up and get married before I can take over any of Pop's business. Being a full-time streamer isn't something that she considers a 'real' job." He flashed up two fingers in a finger quote motion around the word.

That's it! I knew his voice sounded familiar. "What's your name? Your stream name, that is?" Plucking another spoon out from the drawer, I reached down for a second bite and popped the sweet curl into my mouth.

"Chaos, why?" He arched one dark eyebrow high, the strands of vampire red starting to fade from his eyes as they sparkled with something else. Interest. A lot of interest. "Are you a gamer too? What's your name?"

I shook my head, a few strands of hair drifting free of my braid to tickle my cheek. "I'm just your average casual lurker, I don't game anymore, not since I took over my grandparent's cafe. I used to enjoy it a lot, but now I just seem to run out of spare time." Carefully tucking the strands behind my ear, I started to wonder if it was just me, or if the air was really steaming up.

His smile stretched his cheeks so far up that it looked like his face was about to split in half. "No kidding? That's awesome. Lurkers are great supporters too! Hey, you wanna know something?" Chaos's smile quickly shifted from delighted beaming to boyishly impish in a heartbeat. Placing the ice cream tub into the hands of a passing kitchen assistant, he awkwardly hopped off the counter with his legs sprawled almost crab style. "There's a sick game room here in the house, down in the basement. You gotta come see-!"

"Who is that?" I asked, carefully holding my dress up as I slid to my feet. A small tug at my backside sent an instant stab of horror right to my heart. The long rip stretching down the side of my gown didn't help any, opening up this pit of dread in my stomach that was so large it could swallow a limo. I closed my eyes, silently praying that maybe it wasn't as bad as what it sounded like. It could always be a trick of the light, couldn't it?

It wasn't.

Oh, Renae was going to kill me! Starting just above my left hip and going all the way down to mid-calf, a gaping tear in the smooth silk exposed most of my butt and special seamless nude panties for the world to see. I nearly choked on my own spit, fluttering my hands across the damaged material like it might make it magically disappear. "It's my sister! I've got to go!" Chaos hissed, his fangs fully out and his wide eyes vampire red in pure horror. His head whipped side to side, the sapphire flecked tips of his hair swaying like it was doing the mamba, and he started to dash away when I grabbed his arm.

"I've got to hide somewhere until I can get this," I flashed part of the torn fabric up at him. A faint blush crept up his pale cheeks, but none of the other kitchen staff seemed to be paying us the least bit of attention. Blissfully unaware of our presence as they cooked, flambeed, and plated what had to be twenty different meals, I grabbed his arm and started using him for a body shield. "Fixed. My best friend will kill me if I ruin her borrowed dress!"

"Okay, got it. Umm..." He roughly raked a hand through his hair, the carefully styled strands sticking straight up like porcupine quills. "Let's go to the-"

WHAM

"Brother, what in the hell did you do!"

5

When Chaos said that his sister was a hurricane, I honestly wasn't expecting the human equivalent of a Bantam hen with the temper of a Tasmanian Devil on a bad day. Blowing past my own height of 5'5 by a few inches, with a svelte body like a miniature runway model, beauty queen worthy blonde hair teased into the perfect sideswept 'do, and petite features perfectly sculpted in a way that some women couldn't achieve with thousands of dollars of plastic surgery. Chaos's sister was a knockout, and if her perfectly matched scarlet nails to her flowing gown was any indication, her temper was too.

"What did you do to Erica? She called me, threatening to stake me if I so much as even suggested-" She broke off in mid-sentence, her ruby eyes flashing like fire against the smoky grey of her eyeshadow as her glare moved over to me. "Who are you? And why is your dress ripped?"

Chaos cringed against my side like a scolded puppy, all big teary eyes and a quivering lower lip. Anxiously twisting the hem of his shirt between his fingers until I was sure it would rip, his mouth opened and closed, but only a few gurgles managed to make it out. Despite his obvious distress, he shifted forward like he was trying to shield me from his sister's wrath. A surge of protectiveness clawed right through my chest, and I pushed right out to stand in front of him. Planting my hands on my hips, superhero style, I gave his sister one of those bring-it-on-bitch stares right back. "I'm his date for this evening. We were just having a little fun, and I ripped my dress." Using my best sugary sweet irate customer voice, I flashed a conspiratorial wink her way and popped a kiss right on his icy cheek. "You know how it is when you're a little too involved in each other and things just start falling right out of place."

A few garbled sounds echoed from Chaos's throat like he was choking on his tongue, and his eyes almost bulged out of his sockets. His sister paused, openmouthed, and did the weird gape thing just like her brother. It must be a family thing. Finally, once the shock settled in, her ruby eyes started to retreat to a similar but slightly darker shade of honey brown like her brother. "You," She pointed one well-manicured claw at my heart, "are in a relationship with him." The dagger finger switched to Chaos, and his shoulders slumped so far down that he almost melted into a puddle. "Willingly?"

"Yep," I grinned, feeling so proud of myself that this little lie popped right into my head. Usually, I can't think on my feet, Renae is the one that can pop off things like that, but this was worthy of a full page in her book. Lacing my fingers with his, it was a little bit of a shock to feel how cold they were, and just how rough they were too. The traditional corpse cold vampire skin I assumed, but I tried to not let the surprise show on my face as I flashed her another wink. "Is there a place around here where I could fix a little wardrobe malfunction?"

Her whole body jolted like electricity had surged through her flawless frame. "Oh, yes. Yes. Of course. Brother, take her too somewhere private. Very private." She shook her head again like she couldn't believe it, the entire mass of hair not even moving along with her body. Giving us another slightly startled look, she spun on her heel and charged back through the door, nearly clocking a passing waiter right in the stomach if he hadn't leaped back just in time.

"How did- Who- Why- That was awesome!" Jabbering around before finally spitting it out, Chaos wrapped his arms around my waist and lifted me high up into the air above his head. His smile was so broad that his eyes had closed, my hands instantly snapped for a hold on his neck as he started to twirl. The white jackets of the chefs blurred into one big jelly shaped blob as he spun around, also flashing everyone a nice view of my rear through the rip in my dress, but I was too motion sick to complain. My arms were firmly fastened to his neck, so tight that they would have been cutting off his air if he wasn't a vampire and extra sturdy, and my stomach flip-flopped dangerously. "I've never seen anyone handle my sister so well! Not even my mother! You are amazing! Glorious! Wonderful! And- And-"

"And going to be sick if you don't put me down!" Any

"Oops!" He chuckled sheepishly, slowly coming to a stop as his impressive strength lowered me to the ground. His hands came to rest on my shoulders, steadying me while letting his natural coolness seep into my skin. It was a good thing because I couldn't tell what was up or down right now. My fingers stayed curled into the lapels of his jacket until my shoes brushed the floor, my stomach doing a strange combo of the limbo and the samba that left me queasy. "Sorry about that. Sometimes I get a little carried away once I get going." I wasn't complaining, standing this close was giving me a major shot of his cologne, and that was doing miracles for my aching head.

Thick and rich, swirled with rich bourbon and soft vanilla, it was instantly richer than any of the ice cream that I tasted earlier. It did wonders for straightening out the dizziness looping through my head, and I blinked, almost brushing the tip of his nose with mine. The tender warmth in his eyes made my skin feel much too warm, the flecks of gold swirling deep in the amber brown so mesmerizing that I could stare at his eyes all day and never be bored. "It's okay." I finally mumbled, my knees feeling a little shaky like they were about to give out on me at any moment. "I'm alright."

"Come on, let's go somewhere and get your pretty dress all fixed up." His hands slid down from my shoulders to my wrists, the nimble fingers quickly weaving with mine, and he guided me out of the kitchen through a smaller side door. Destination unknown.

6

As Chaos led me down a dark stairwell and deeper into this sprawling mansion, a tiny trickle of fear started to nag away at my mind until it started to flood with doubt. Maybe I shouldn't have been so quick to follow an unknown vampire into an unfamiliar place. What if he was starving for something more than the desert he was eating previously? Or if he was one of those strange ones that still liked to hunt and feed off of unwilling victims? He didn't have that kind of air around him. If anything, he acted more like a puppy.

And the nice view of his shapely tuxedo clad rump sauntering in front of me wasn't half bad either.

"Hey, you okay?" I blinked, the soft lighting from the rounded lamps above threw dark shadows around everything below my waist. Chaos had paused three steps away, his left hand still holding on to the elegantly carved wooden banister running parallel along the wall, and his plush lips were pursed slightly in a small pout of concern. "I know the steps are a little scary, but I promise I'm not a serial killer or anything. I don't drink blood straight from the vein. No one in my family has for years." His gaze slipped to the side like something had just popped in his head, a light frown creating a thick v crease between his brows. "Well, except when Dad gets a little feisty with one of his lady friends."

"Oh... thanks, I guess." My cheeks flushed, feeling a little like the stupid heroine in a bad horror movie, and I started inching down the steps again. The suffocating weight of the silence broke as he started humming lightly under his breath, a cheery little tune that reminded me of a game I used to play, and the knot in my chest started to ease. That's when I noticed that the soft squeaks of his shoes bouncing off the polished wood flooring changed. Becoming deeper, like the steps beneath his feet were growing more solid. A few more steps, and the vague frame of an open door slowly materialized in the gloom.

"Here we are! The game room of the Von Dracula estate!" Chaos vanished to one side, flipping a few switches as I stepped down onto the last step. A series of rainbow tube shaped lamps running from wall to ceiling lit up on command, bathing the room in a soft glow. Not too dark or too bright, it was just perfect for the limitations of the small room. Picking up the soft undertones of lavender in the periwinkle walls, the cozy atmosphere felt even softer by the long plush black leather sofa stretching just to my left, piled thick with so many plushies that it looked like a toy store had exploded. The sofa faced a slender flat screen tv braced to the opposite wall, a 43 inch by my rough estimate, and underneath it was a wide assortment of the latest game consoles currently made.

My gaze wandered over to the right where an impatiently shuffling Chaos was shyly smiling as he held his arms wide, presenting a large L-shaped white desk with three large monitors, keyboard, and a set of wireless headphones that were padded for extra comfort. More streaming items like a cylindrical mike, camera, and a phone rest in case someone wanted to use their phone as a stream deck was scattered about the top. I couldn't see underneath the desk very well from this angle, and the space occupied by the comfortable chair, but the multiple blinking lights looked like it was all top-quality tech living under there as well.

"Wow! This is a sweet setup!" Whoever had outfitted this room had some major money tied up in it. Which made sense since this was the Von Dracula mansion we were standing in. Picking the hem of my gown up slightly, I shuffled over to the sofa and pushed a few plushies aside with my hip, sinking down into the cloud like fluffiness with a small groan. A few minutes more, and I wouldn't be leaving this sofa for anything. "Normally I would appreciate it, but right now I really need to fix my gown so my best friend doesn't kill me for ruining it."

"Oh, yeah! Here, I know someone who can whip that up for you really quick, no sweat. Wait just a second!" Twisting around so fast that his tuxedo jacket started slipping halfway down his slender shoulders, Chaos landed in the desk chair and rolled over to the keyboard. With his long fingers flashing like lightning, the light from several screens quickly flashed over his face. Illuminating the little dimple in the corner of his left cheek and the long slope of his nose, my heart did a weird little flutter at how cute the level of intense focus was in his eyes. He really needed to include a camera on his streams.

"You want something?"

I screamed, grabbed a huge chicken shaped plushie, and battered the phantom head that popped out of the wall. It didn't stop, sailing right through the high domed forehead and the flat top haircut with ease. A series of black x-shaped stitches extended the sides of both lips up nearly to its ears, and the bulging fish-like eyes were red rimmed against the sallow blue skin. "What the hell are you?" I screamed again, swinging the plushie like it was a hammer. The creepy ghost thing just rolled his eyes, a sorrowful moan gurgling in the patchwork throat.

"Hey! Don't beat up Hans! He's a good guy!" A dark blur dashed in front of my eyes, and suddenly five long fingers were delicately holding my wrist up. Gently keeping me from punching Ye Olde Creepy Voodoo Ghost, Chaos hopped up on the couch with his bony knees spread on either side of my hips, pinning my arm above my head while the other was spread against his chest. My fingers curled deep into the silk, tugging down one corner of his shirt and waistcoat to reveal a slice of toned shoulder and the shimmering curve of the dragon's neck. "Don't be scared, okay?" His honey eyes glistened with a confidence that was missing earlier, and my head nodded without my control. Scared was thrown right out the window along with all of my reasonable thoughts, my mind was completely goo.

With his body hovering just inches above my own, it was too easy to feel the icy chill leaking from his frame. Compared to his body, his breath was warm as it fanned across my face, and still sweetened from the ice cream from earlier. I blinked, the tip of my tongue darting out to edge along my lower lip, and his gaze quickly dropped to follow it. Well, crap. A once very distant but intimately familiar warmth started to curl down below, something that I hadn't experienced in quite a while. My breath hitched, arching my chest just a little higher than normal, and his throat bobbed as he swallowed heavily. Apparently, I wasn't the only one feeling this way.

"You want something, sir?" The ghost repeated, skeletal bony fingers idly pulling at a loose stitch running up its cheek.

Chaos's body twitched like he couldn't really believe it. "Yeah, how fast can those fingers of yours sew up a pretty gown like this?" Within the space of a breath, he was gone. Slipping down to sit beside me, Chaos lifted the ripped edge of my gown closest to my feet and flashed it towards the ghost. My left hand flared to my chest, trying to contain my pounding heart, and I struggled to breath properly.

The bulging eyes rolled, one briefly looking in each direction before finally focusing on the Grand Canyon-like rip showing off my leg. He groaned, slowly lifting one hand palm out, and a travel size sewing kit popped right into his palm. "May I have the dress?" The butler muttered.

"Do you have something else I could put on?" Hugging my arms close to my chest in case Mr. Creepy decided to try and spirit my dress off, a flash of movement out of the corner of my right eye caught my attention. Chaos, bent over the desk with his shapely butt turned straight up in the air, was rummaging through something stored on the opposite side of the desk. Slowly shifting his slender hips from side to side like a happy golden retriever, I couldn't tell if I wanted to laugh or blush from ogling just how well his trousers were fitting to each curve of his nicely shaped rear.

"Here we go!" He suddenly shouted out, bouncing up from across the desk with a triumphant smile like he had just won an award. One hand held a baggy black t-shirt in, and a pair of faded jeans dangled from the other, both items slightly worn around the edges but well loved. Were they his or someone else's? "I think this will fit you. Not as nice as your pretty dress, but- Oh, shit! Did I say that out loud?" Bulging out almost as bad as the butler's, Chaos's shining eyes widened so far that they nearly popped out of his skull, and the brilliant flush returned to his cheeks brighter than ever. I didn't even know vampires could blush that much. "I'm sorry! So sorry! I didn't mean to be creepy.

Here!" He threw the clothes straight across the room into my lap, although the shirt sailed right above my head and smacked against the wall. "We'll step out of here and let you change. Sorry again!"

"It's okay!" I shot back, but he was stumbling towards the door too quickly to understand. His legs all tangled together like limp noodles, he tilted forward face first towards the floor, but managed to recover at the last second. The door slammed shut behind him, a second, much harsher, thump came from the opposite side of the door. I started to wonder if maybe he fell and hurt himself, but a few curses drifted through the door after all. Mr. Creepy groaned low and loud, dismissively shaking his head as he floated through the door in pursuit. I hope Chaos was okay, he was very sweet even if he was a little clumsy. And he smelled so nice too.

It hit me like a bullet as I was trying to slide out of my gown with the least amount of damage to the silky fabric possible. He made me laugh. That's something no guy has been able to do in... I don't know when. That and get my inner mojo going. I know I should be upstairs, floating with all the movers and shakers, but maybe it wouldn't hurt to stay here for a few more minutes. At least until the butler had sewn up my dress.

7

"Ooo, cool! Space Fighters 9. That's a rare one." Trailing my fingertips over the slender case of the game, the extra bold yellow title was certainly tempting to pop into the game console, but it was just one of many little gems hidden in a small clear storage cube in the corner of the room. I thought that once I was dressed and had handed my gown over to the mercy of Mr. Voodoo's floating hand through the door, Chaos might come back but so far it was just me, myself, and I browsing through the extensive game library. I started to reach for a second title in a vibrant blue and yellow box, but the sagging sleeve of my borrowed shirt decided to take that moment and flop all the way down to my fingertips. Darn sleeve! I sighed, rolling the too long material back up to my elbows when I heard a shy little knock at the door.

"H-Hey! I'm back with some goodies. Are you ready?" Tentative and slightly muffled, I hopped up from where I had been sitting on the floor, nearly tripped over the hem of my baggy jeans pooling around my ankles, and rushed to open the door. Standing on the other side was Chaos, but he had slipped out of his fancy tuxedo somewhere along the way. Replaced by a black hoodie two sizes too large, and a pair of jeans just barely clinging to his hips, his arms were loaded with two large carryout containers, and topped with a smaller one with a clear domed lid. "Hey! You're dressed. Awesome!" A warm glow brought out the flecks of gold in the honey brown, the fine skin crinkling at the corners with a smile that I couldn't see behind the teetering tower of takeout. "I've got a few goodies to snack on while I was gone."

"Cool. How's Mr. Creepy Voodoo doing with my gown." Keeping the door open with my hip, I lifted the smallest container off the top, and scooted back to let him by. Chaos waddled on through, his blue tinged hair bobbing playfully with every step, and made his way to the desk to relieve his burden.

"He's doing pretty well. You probably couldn't tell by how he looks, but he's a real master with a needle." Carefully placing each container aside like it was made of gold, he popped the lid on a larger one, his shoulders swelling up as he sucked in a deep breath. I glanced down at the container in my hand, and saw two slabs of some kind of pinkish meat that vaguely resembled rubber. I swallowed heavily, bile starting to surge in my throat at the thought of even putting one single morsel in my mouth. Oh, wonderful... meat. "One of the kitchen workers said that someone brought in a huge chocolate cherry blood cake for the vampires. A real work of baked art, and it smelled so good that I snuck out a couple slices. I know you're a human and all, so I got you a slice of the big chocolate part safe from all the blood ingredients." He turned, popping off the lid of the container with a flourish worthy of a Las Vegas showroom. "Tah-dah! The most beautiful chocolate cake in the world!"

Lovingly nestled into the secure plastic container were two slices of cake that I had spent hours decorating to perfection. Elegantly twirled rosettes of the deepest fudge rose up like peaks from the base of the rich buttercream frosting, each one topped by a shiny red maraschino cherry. Long stemmed, of course. Layer after layer of frosting cascaded down the outer edge of the slice, creating a delicate basket weave effect that I had painstakingly piped along the sides. More swirls of fudge had twined up and down the layers like vines, and the slices he had still included a nice chunk of my work as well. The deep dark chocolate cake layers were fluffy as air instead of the dense layer that most people were expecting, tinted with the cherry liquor in both layers, but the one with the extra hint of blood was usually undetectable by humans in scent. Vampires were certainly different based on how plump his pupils were swelling up, and a little pride welled up inside me from knowing that all my hard work and calculations had produced a mouthwatering dessert that both species could enjoy.

"I'm glad you like my work." Taking care to slide beside him and placing the container of meat on the desk, I muffled my giggle behind the pop of the second lid releasing into my hand. A flood of fresh steam quickly bathed my face, the spicy scent of fresh steamed vegetables seasoned with ginger and something else. A little sweet, like honey, but with a touch of something extra. A little pungent. I closed my eyes, taking in a long whiff, and let the scent dance around my senses. Orange peel! That was it!

"Oh... You made this? This is freaking awesome! You've got to be the best baker around!" The beaming smile couldn't have been any brighter if he tried, bouncing over to the couch and folding his legs up criss cross style, Chaos balanced the container of cake on his knee and motioned me to sit. "Pop in whatever you want to play, and let's see if you've got what it takes to beat me."

"You got it!" Throwing my hand up in a mock salute, I popped the cover back over the vegetables, pushed it back on the desk, and walked over to grab the first combat style game that my fingers found. An adventure RPG over an exotic land with a trainable dragon pet, it sounded totally awesome and my hand practically guided itself over to the console.

Popping the game into the slot, a few beeps and a series of lights flashed across the top as the tongue-like tray was sucked back in. I shuffled back on my knees, the whirling hum of the console clicking into life drowning out the slight squeak as I flopped back on the couch. Chaos passed me the container and a fork, taking a huge bite of the fudge icing himself, and the moan that followed made my toes curl. "Oh, this is so *good*." It was all throaty whispers and scorching warmth, my hands trembling to hold the container as an unfamiliar heat settled low in my core. He moaned again, just as seductive as the first time, and my eyes restlessly shifted to the side.

Ho-ly shit!

The back of his head rested against the curve of the sofa, exposing the beautiful line of his throat, and the sapphire tipped strands mushed back into a beautiful disheveled mess. His eyes were completely closed, long feathery lashes flaring over his cheeks, and his chocolate-stained lips curved up slightly higher on one corner versus the other. He swallowed heavily, the slight bulge of his Adam's apple dancing temptingly up and down in his throat. Damn, I'm not even a vampire and I would love to run my teeth up and down the length of his throat. I blinked, turning back around to face the screen, but the deep thumping bass music and quick combat intro only made my heart feel like it was about to slam through my chest. Or drop all the way down to the soft ache slowly growing stronger between my thighs.

"I-I take it you like it?" Damn it! I couldn't do this. This wasn't me. I didn't want to straddle the first random guy that moaned while eating my cake. Hell, I haven't even been in a relationship to actually get that far in forever. Shifting my focus down to the controls, the different shaped buttons all blurred together. Trying to control my breathing into something that wasn't a rapid pant, something unfamiliar quickly stopped me. A tentative poke against my thigh, the bones in my neck cracking stiffly, and turned to see Chaos positively beaming like he was a ray of sunshine, one that had a mask of chocolate frosting caked around his lips. "My grandma would be proud. It was her recipe for the cake layers, I just tweaked it a bit."

"This is seriously the best dessert I have ever had! She must have been one hell of a cook! Have you tasted it?" I shook my head, not entirely trusting my tongue to talk right now, and he wasn't satisfied in the least. "Oh, come on. You gotta try it! Here!" One long finger swiped through the fudge icing, the fat blob barely clinging to the tip and threatening to fall off at any moment.

"No! That's okay!" The control fell against the floor with a dull thud as my hands flared up, palms out and fingers spread wide to block off any further advances. I really didn't want any now. After spending so many hours decorating the thing down to the very last swirl, the last thing I wanted right now was a taste of the chocolate overload. "I don't eat sweets that I bake. Usually, I can barely just stand the smell of it by the time I'm through."

"Oh. Sorry." Like a popped balloon, Chaos started to deflate from some of that joy. His shoulders slumped down, the glossy sheen quickly fading from his bright eyes, and he cautiously lowered his hand down to rest on his lap. "You must have really loved her a lot, because it shows in how well you've baked. That's an art that can't be faked ya know?"

I nodded again. A quick flash of white teeth caught the corner of my eye, and my gaze dropped to where his teeth were nervously nibbling at his chocolate covered lower lip. Then his gaze flashed up to meet mine, the soft flecks of gold darkening to a beautiful amber. I sucked in a harsh breath, my gaze falling to his lip and then back up, and he followed every motion. Sweat quickly starts rolling down my neck, the temperature of the room rising up a few more degrees, and I can't tell if it's just me or if he's feeling it too. Like someone was pulling me on a string, I started to lean forward, stretching one hand out to brace myself on his lap-

"Oh, shit!" A sharp pain lanced right through my finger, cutting right through the bone and out the other side. My arm snapped back to my chest, the fork he was eating with was still impaled dead center of my pointer finger, a thick river of crimson flowing down the sides. More pearl sized droplets snaked down my wrist in thin winding trails, clinging to the underside of my palm before dripping off to splatter against Chaos's thigh. I started to apologize, clutching my bleeding finger between my good one when I heard a small hiss. Then came the groan, so thick and deep that my hair stood on end and my thighs started to anxiously rub together without my control. I looked up, and what I saw took my breath away.

8

"You okay?" He asked softly, but the seductive way the vampiric red starts to bleed into the honey brown of his irises left me thinking I might be anything but. Chaos leaned over, the loose material of his hoodie not quite disguising the ripple of muscles beneath his skin, and plucked the fork away with two long fingers. I barely felt the sting, too lost in the way his fingers trailed over the broken skin like the blood was nothing at all. "Damn. That looks like it hurts. Let me go get a few bandages. Here" He pushed a few paper napkins against my cut, folding my own fingers around the wound and gently encouraging me to press down. "Hold a little pressure on that and I'll be right back."

Before I could even blink, he had sped away so fast that a puff of wind stirred up in his wake, whipping up a few free strands of hair to slap me right in the face. I sighed, glancing down at the red stain quickly soaking through the white paper. That's going to be sore tomorrow.

BEEP-BEEP

My butt started vibrating in time with the beeping, and I nearly jumped right off the sofa. What was the alarm clock doing on? It usually only beeps at midnight to remind me when I need to stop working. Wedging the blood-soaked napkin between two fingers to keep the pressure on, I leaned up on one hip and jammed my free hand down into the saggy pockets running along my backside. The jittering edge of the phone quickly met my fingertips, shaking like some kind of possessed cha-cha dancer, and a quick two fingered snag flopped it out on my leg. The proud letters of 12:02 a.m. stood out in bright blue across my phone's screen, reminding me not only was it way past my normal business hours, but that I still had to be back at my cafe at 5:00 a.m. for the breakfast rush.

"Double crap! I've got to go, and Mr. Creepy hasn't come back with my dress yet!" Shoving the phone back down into my pocket, I straightened up and swung my legs fully down to the floor. Standing up in one smooth motion, I started to pull the gunky bandage off, and what came off was the little scab that had formed with it. Deep scarlet blood started to flood down my wrist again, playing off the ridges of my veins, and pooling in the curves of my palm. "How can this mess really smell so good?" I wondered, taking the edge of my finger and tracing a small circle through the widest part. It was warm and sticky, the bleeding already starting to slow some, but the ragged gash in my finger was still leaking heavily. A flap of skin flared out from the side, running parallel with my fingernail, but it wasn't as deep as I first thought. Just maybe right under the surface, enough of a poke to bleed but not like a serious injury.

"It smells wonderful, more than you could ever imagine." I jumped, my heart leaping up into my throat, as Chaos padded-No, *prowled*, into the room. The full length of his fangs had sharpened behind his full lips, the white tips fully visible as he flashed an embarrassed smile that left his cheeks flushed and his eyes glittering with hunger. His legs were shaking from the effort to keep still, rolling up onto the balls of his feet before slowly lowering back down. "Something that a lot of people don't realize is that a person's blood is influenced by their personality. Like if you're very aggressive, your blood will taste extra salty. Or if you're more of a thinker, it takes on a subtle fruity flavor." He stopped, his chest swelling up with a single deep breath, and the hoodie didn't seem quite as baggy as before. "You smell very sweet, lightly fruity. Like a peach tart is the best way I could describe it."

"Oh, I had no idea." My blood smelled like a peach tart. That was interesting to know. Twisting my fingers slightly, a fresh round of blood started leaking out from the puncture, and my nose wrinkled up in response. "Okay, more blood. Can you hand me the bandages you got really quick? I hate to leave, but I still have to work in the morning."

"You do?" He started to pull something from the pocket of his hoodie, twitching fingers visible straight through the fabric against his belly, but stopped. "W-Would you-" Chaos broke off, roughly clearing his throat into his fist to hide the tremble in his voice. "I mean, since you need to go. I might be able to help with the bleeding. If you don't mind."

"Really?" One eyebrow arched up so high that I could feel it brush the roots of my hair. Chaos nodded, the flickering hunger in his eyes burning higher as he slunk forward on soundless steps. My gaze firmly glued to his blushing cheeks as he stopped just shy of stepping on my toes, so close that the intense wave of his cologne assaulted my senses so strongly that my head spun. Slowly he lifted one hand from his hoodie, the square edge of the paper napkins hanging out of the very top, and gracefully extended it towards me. He didn't move, not even blinking and barely daring to breathe, as he waited for my silent permission.

It felt like a dream, the arm that lifted wasn't really mine, and the way his long, chilled fingers so securely wrapped around mine wasn't really there. I wasn't sure what to expect, maybe some kind of vampire magic, but the seductive press of his plush lips against my finger was certainly more than enough to make my breathing hitch. The cool wet length of his tongue slowly darted out, lazily lapping around the tip with small kitten licks gently gliding over the ragged edge. His fangs were sharp, lightly grazing against my skin, but it didn't hurt. Our eyes met, my breath starting to sharpen as the inky darkness of his pupils swelled with delight, the vampire ruby red quickly shrinking into just the thinnest rim. He groaned, a small sound like a puppy whimpering, but I felt it roll straight up from the depths of his throat.

"I take it you like the way I taste." I breathed out; my chest so tight that it felt like my bones would break at any moment. A few strands of the longer strands of hair had started to droop forward over his eyes, the brighter tips glowing slightly in the reflection of his eyes. I giggled, starting to feel a little light headed, and pushed the strand back up. His hair was so soft despite whatever he used to keep it pushed up, briefly twisting my fingertips deeper into the waves, and Chaos let out a shuddering breath. He broke away with a sigh, still keeping my hand cradled in his grasp, but his eyes immediately fluttered closed.

"I haven't tasted anything so sweet in centuries." His voice was lower, richer. The seductive curl of his accent thicker as it glazed over every letter from his lips like it was a work of art. My heart started to pound as he leaned in close, letting the sweet ache drift lower and lower to pool between my thighs. My hand flexed, the torn skin no longer bleeding but a healthy blushed pink. The cut was completely gone. My eyes widened, slowly turning my hand around in his grasp, but there wasn't the slightest trace of an imperfection at all. There's no way that was possible. It was completely healed. "I take it you haven't heard about how vampires have a special ingredient in our saliva that can heal a lot of wounds." He chuckled softly, the tip of his slick pink tongue sliding along the rim of his lower lip.

A soft moan crept out of my throat, dark images quickly flashing through my head of where and what he could do with that tongue would be called X-rated at best. "No, I haven't." He lowered his hand to rest against my hip, two fingers tentatively rubbing the shirt hem back and forth between them. "I want you to know something." I said, glancing back up into those magnetic eyes that were so warm and soft despite the feral hunger glowing in the depths.

"What's that?" He did the little head tip thing again, a few more strands of hair giving up the fight and falling across his eyes. My left hand twitched, aching to make a mess of the rest of his hair. And his neck, his neck would look lovely with a ring of bite marks around it.

"I don't normally sleep with guys I just met."

This brought out a laugh that sent shivers crawling all the way down my spine and out to the tips of my toes, but it was the good kind. "Me neither. But there's something different about you. Likes you're a beautiful star and I'm just the fool that got trapped in your light." He answered honestly, his gaze slowly raking over every inch of my body from head to toe and then back again. My spine arched instinctively, pressing my chest forward like he had pulled some invisible string. The ache grew sharper between my legs, the denim unmistakably rustled from my thighs pressing so sharply together, and my cheeks flushed again. How could anyone be so cute and sexy at the same time? That's when he dipped his head, the pointed edge of his chin brushing against his chest, and his shoulders swelled with the effort of his breath. Chaos inhaled sharply, taking in every scrap of my scent in that single breath, and the hunger flared again in his eyes, but it was different this time.

This time it was fueled by lust, his hips subtly gyrating against my thigh, and his impressive length was too easy to feel behind his pants. The cords of muscle started to bulge in his neck, visibly restraining himself from making another move. He was leaving the final decision to me.

How could I say no to that? I reached out, swiftly curling my arms around his neck, and pulled him down for a powerful kiss.

9

His lips were cold, but soft. Still lightly sweet from the cake and tinged with the iron taste of blood, it was nothing like kissing a corpse. Nothing at all, more like a very chilly human. I smiled into the kiss, letting it deepen by parting my lips and brushing my tongue against the seam of his lips. He broke away with a fluttering moan, quickly dropping his forehead to rest against mine l. My eyes slid open, quickly finding his own that were so dilated that the dark pupil looked coin sized against the ruby red rim. "H-Hey," he chuckled softly, his fingertips lightly skimming over my shoulder, and a flash of white teeth nibbled along his lower lip. I shivered, the ghost of his touch sparking fireworks beneath my skin. So light it's barely there, it drifts up my jaw, the rounded pad of his thumb reverently stroking my skin like I'm something fragile he might break. My body leans into his touch, the coolness not so surprising now, and my hands fist into his hoodie. He jolts slightly in surprise, the brief contact of my breasts smashing against his chest drive his hips forward, and his nostril flare with the barely suppressed hard breath.

"Hey," I whispered back, my stomach nearly driving up right up in my throat as my left hand dropped to press against his stomach. The loose fabric can't disguise the firm skin beneath, and it easily slides away as my fingers explore, teasing the small slice of exposed skin above his waistband. He flinches, a few choked gurgles leaking out of his throat, and all the momentary confidence he had vanishes as the red flush spreads all the way down his neck. "You okay?"

"F-Fine," A second brush of my fingertips over the subtle curve of his soft abs, he shuddered heavily, breathing sharp and quick as his eyes clenched tight. Like a wall that's starting to break, he leans forward into my touch, and props one hand on each side of my head. He's beautiful even now, his hair and face a blushing, stuttering mess, and I wonder how much more he could take if I reach lower. Pressing my palm flat, my hand slides down, curling around the hard bulge that's tenting his jeans out and flaring out for a tentative stroke. The fabric beside my ear rips apart, his clenched fingers ripping deep furrows in the leather surface, and his breath stops. "I-I'm just really sensitive to touch." It's too easy to see how heavily his throat bulges when he swallows, his eyes opening just a slit, and he tries to wink. My hips shift, rubbing my thighs together against the press of his knee, and it feels so good that I can't stop.

"Is that a bad thing?" I started to pull my hand away, but a flash of motion pins it underneath the fabric before I could even draw a breath.

"No," Chaos growled, his eyes flashing fully open again. Those dark eyes, the single word broke something in him. The jagged shards of the wall crashing down can't disguise the hot hunger thrumming through his veins. My heart pounds, slamming against my ribs, and I'm sure he can hear it. I know he can hear it because he squeezes my hand and spreads it fully over the soft flesh of his belly. "Don't move."

With his growl still ringing in my ears, my hand stays perfectly poised in the curved indentation of his pecs. His body rippled, muscles flexing and twisting as he whipped the hoodie off and tossed it to some forgotten corner to be found later. He's beautiful, all soft skin speckled with little freckles the color of butterscotch, and the full length of the dragon lazily sprawls out over his skin. With the long head and neck starting just below his jawline, the long snake-like body curls down, looping over his left shoulder and down around his ribcage. The narrow tail slinks out of sight, curving around his back to end at the opposite of his right hip. It's beautiful, much larger than I thought it would be, but complements his skin so nicely. My eyes trace over every inch of him, the heaving of his chest growing sharper with every breath, and the ache between my thigh's doubles in strength. Including the slight dampness soaking my underwear. "You're really handsome, you know that?" He blinks, almost like he couldn't believe I said so, and his frame melts into my touch.

"Glad you think so," His cheeks flush bright red again, now spreading down his chest as my other hand comes up to rest on his shoulder. Leaning in, I tip my head just enough that his nose brushes mine, crushing my breasts to his chest, and angling in for a kiss on those lips. The hard line of his jaw is what greets me instead, and I start to scowl before he lets some of his weight drop down. The frame squeaks in protest, bracing himself up with an arm returning on either side of my head, and the rounded curve of his knee tentatively but firmly presses just right between my thighs. "But I think that it's you who's really the gorgeous one." His breath is hot, too hot as it fans across my skin, and it feels like I'm melting.

Slowly, almost reverently, his cool hands ghost down my body. His dark gaze flicking up every now and then for reassurance, and I nod woodenly because my tongue refuses to work. He leans back on his knees, letting his fingertips wander over the slope of my chest and curl around my breasts. I breathe out a sigh when they tug against the hardened peak of my nipples, and his lips quickly follow the same path. Sticky, openmouthed kisses litter the fabric across my chest, the chill of his touch does nothing against the sweat starting to paste the shirt to my skin, and I need it off. Now! My hands start tugging at my shirt like something possessed, on the verge of ripping the fabric away when a firm hand stops my own.

"Need a little help?" Those magic fingertips trace a path down my ribs, curving up under the hem, and finding bare skin. The rough calluses on the pads of his fingers tease, goosebumps quickly blooming over my skin, and I can't breathe right when they tease against the tight band of my bra. The clinging fabric quickly gives away under his touch, flying over his shoulder to join his hoodie somewhere else. My bra goes too, flying through the air in a nude-colored bundle. The sudden absence is freeing, but I've never felt more naked than the way his gaze traveled over my breasts. The hungry grin swells, bleeding into pure lust, and he shifts his knee. The sudden spike of pressure against my sensitive core was too much, ripping a screech right out of my throat. My hands fly to his body for support, raking my nails down his chest, and my hips frantically bucking up in search of more pressure. The rasp of the jean seam created the most beautiful contrast of pleasure and pain, tightening up a coil deep in my core, and my breath leaks out with a shaky moan.

Feather light, his fingers swirl across the peaks of my nipples. Light, gentle, but with just enough tease that it makes my spine arch. Chaos continued down, his palm flat against my stomach and still sliding lower, and lower before finally dipping beneath the waistband of my jeans. Lifting my hands up, they curl through the thick strands of his hair, and pauses just long enough for a delighted purr to leak out of his chest. I'm too impatient to wait, my grip tightening, and his kiss swollen lips round into a soft o. He doesn't stay like that for long, a man returning to his mission with a strength that defied my expectations. One hand slid under my butt, so eager for his touch that my hips buck, and every inch of my focus narrows on those fingers whipping the fabric away and teasing the fringes of my lower curls. "Damn, it feels good!" His coolness and the nimble strength, the slightly rough edge of his callouses against the soft tender skin. It's all so good that my fingers curl into his hair, one hand wandering up and down the smooth flesh of his back, and the pudding soft flesh of his stomach.

"You like that?" I nodded, my tongue too knotted up to speak and my head flops back against the couch. "Good. I thought maybe we were going too fast for you." His eyes never leave my face, so focused like I was the only thing in the world that mattered to him. The intensity of his eyes made my stomach shiver, or maybe that was the pulse of his fingers sliding in and out of my slick core. I don't need vampire senses to hear the obscene wet squelch, and a tight knot starts to pull in my core when his thumb presses just right against my clit. I start to return the favor, reaching down to cup my hands against the length of his clothed cock, but the tips barely brush the hot length before he knocks my grasp away with his elbow. "Not just yet," He whispers low, dipping his head down to where his lips hovered just over my breast. "I've got a few more ideas I want to see first."

My hand slaps over my mouth to muffle the scream, the soft fringe of his hair tickling my chest as he sucks my nipple into his mouth. His fingers move in sync with his lips, sliding through my folds and pumping lightly. It doesn't take much to have me on the verge of losing my mind. The added press of his hips grinding down against mine doesn't help, even with his hand trapped between us, I can still feel the all too clear outline of his cock throbbing against my core.

A second finger slips in, along with him switching his attention to my abandoned breast, changes things on a dime. My breathing sharpens, my hands grasping onto the edge of the sofa for support, and my eyes fly wide open as he circles a thumb around my clit. Circling, weaving, pumping in a steady dance that pulls me closer to the edge. He groans as my core shivers around him, the steady muscles of his back shifting under my hands as he grinds harder, aching for a release of his own pleasure. Something high pitched and screeching claws at my ears, almost inhumane sounding, but it's leaking from my lips, and it spurs him on. Driving faster and further, his lips pull back in a snarl, the razor-sharp edge of his teeth dragging across my skin feels like tiny lightning bolts. Chaos climbs up, smothering my lips in a formless kiss, and adds a third finger to the heady mix.

I can't take it. My head tosses back, my groans mixing with his, and white explodes behind my eyes. Several versions of his name slip past my lips, but they're stolen away as my climax explodes full force. Riding away on the waves of bliss, it takes a few moments for me to come back to myself, but when I do. It's to that shy killer smile that ties my core up in a knot.

"Ready to go again?

10

I blinked, slowly watching the ceiling shift into focus as his lips lazily trail down my neck. The sharp tips of his fangs just barely grazed over my pulse; a shiver rolled down the jellied length of my spine. He shifts, a momentary draft of cool air sweeping across my chest, and my damp nipples perk up even harder. "You are so pretty." Chaos whispers, his accent grates like gravel as his hips lazily drag up and down against my thigh. The wet length of his tongue swirling down across my chest, somewhere in my foggy head it registers that he intends to go down the same path again, but I want something different. I have to have something different, like him inside me, because I can't take another round of his magic tongue or I'll break into a thousand pieces.

"Come here!" I growled, threading my fingers through his hair, and tugging so sharply that he let out a long moan. His eyes flutter shut, the entire weight of his body dropping limp against mine. Twisting out of his grasp, it's easy to push him right over onto his back. Just a quick press of my hips and a twist to his arm, and over he goes. A predatory growl rises in his chest, his hands latching on to my hips and digging in sharply while his eyes slowly slid open. The ruby shade darkens as I swallow back a moan, trying to keep myself from grinding down on his cock trapped between our bodies. His jeans are gone, tossed away while I was blacked out, and now there's nothing but cool bare skin pressed against mine. I haven't got a good look at it yet, but the silky feel of him just outside of where I need him most has me dripping wet even more. "Good boy," I meant it as a complement, but he blushed as if it meant something more.

"H-Hang on!" An experimental twitch of my hips made his eyes roll back in his head, his fingers holding my skin so tightly that I'd have bruises tomorrow. "M-My jeans!" The curve of his throat flexed heavily, but speech didn't seem possible at the moment. Closing his eyes, I felt the muscles in his chest shift under my hands as he started to try again. "Condom! In my wallet!" Ah! There we go! I can't believe I was so stupid to forget that. I should slap myself, but the insistent press of his cock against my folds snapped my mind back to what he said.

"Gotcha. Coming right up." A tingling buzz of excitement bloomed in my chest as I swung my legs off his lap, but they didn't offer much support as I wobbled over to the pile of discarded clothes. Like I was walking on two cups of pudding, each step felt like a mile long, and the end was just barely drifting into sight. A quick search through the pile, and my fingers were shaking so badly that I could barely search his pockets, much less finally unfold his thick leather wallet and find the little foil wrapped square stored behind his credit cards. "Do you want to do it or me?" I asked, the shiny wrapper quickly shredding beneath my nails.

"I-I'll do it!" Chaos said, but he didn't seem inclined to move at all. Fully leaned back against the sofa with his legs slightly spread apart, the full heavy weight of his flushed cock rested right against his freckled stomach. His chest heaved with every breath, the pink flush spreading all the way from his cheeks to his chest, and speckled with the collar of red bites around his neck. His eyes vaguely followed my movements as I wobbled my way back to him, fingers restlessly twitching like shockwaves were rolling under his skin when I finally managed to pass it to him, and he rolled it down his length. "Come here." He curls a finger up, calling me forward, but just like him. I had a few ideas I wanted to try.

Taking a careful seat on his knees, he shivers at the feel of my damp lips against his thigh, and I reach out and cup my fingers around his length. First one, then a second pass all the way from head to root brings him to life. A ragged hiss leaks between his pressed lips, his back arching so far that the back of his head presses against the curve of the sofa. "J-Just... There! Yes!" He's not quiet in the least, veins and tendons standing out in sharp contrast along the curve of his neck as he moans, and I added a little extra twist of my wrist to the pumping action of my hand. I swear it looks like he is going to come right there, the ragged gasps partially muffled by the hand he slaps across his mouth. My core throbs with an aching need, and I can't stand it any longer. My opposite hand slips between my folds, keeping time with the buck of his hips. "Good boy, such a good boy. You feel so good!" I wasn't sure if he really heard the words fall out of my mouth, but the bruising grip on my hips tightens. He heard every word.

He swallows hard as I slide my knees on either side of his hips, lifting up just enough to guide him right in, and my head falls back on my own shoulders at the feel of finally getting what I needed. Maybe it was the buzz from my earlier orgasm, or just the heat of the moment, but I let out a breathy laugh as the entire girth of his cock stretched me out so *well*. He slid right in, hot and hard against the softness of my core. I leaned down, using the leverage of my knees to slowly pump up and down his length, and pressed my lips to his. His lips parted easily, tongue eagerly darting forward to slide against my own. One hand curled up and around my neck, nimble fingers twining deep in my hair, and he tugged softly. Baring the left side of my neck, the smooth flesh ripples under my hand as he leans up and presses his forehead to my shoulder.

"Would you... allow me a taste?" It's so soft I barely catch it, but it takes my foggy mind a moment to catch up with the words he whispered into my skin. A taste? That means a bite, right? His hips slowly buck against mine, the push and pull of his cock sliding almost all the way out before coming back again. Even though I'm on top, he's using his strength to keep the pace steady, just the way I need it most. Arching my left leg higher against the right side of his ribs, I leaned down in silent permission to let him do what he wanted. His breath quickens, surprise etched into every hungry line of his expression, and his thrusts sharpen. "Thank you," Chaos whispers like it's a prayer, ghosting his lips over my collarbone with just the faintest hint of teasing fangs.

"No more teasing! Just bite me already!" His pace quickened on command, the lewd slap of damp skin meeting skin. I tried to bite back a moan, my hands flying to his shoulders for a hold, but there's no keeping back the breathless whines that leak out with every one of his thrusts. Sucking a path up my neck, his left hand splayed behind my shoulders and kept me pressed entirely against him. I shuddered, twisting my neck further into his grasp.

Then he bit. His twin fangs plunged into my neck like blazing hot knives. I screamed, fingers curling down to bite into the thicker fleshy skin of his shoulders as the steady lapping of his tongue pulls the blood from my wound. The heady smell of sex and blood made my head spin, I'd never imagined myself being one that would enjoy something like this, but the wet smack of his lips and the throbbing heat between my thighs tipped me over the edge. A strangled cry that was half scream, half a mumbled mess of his name left me gasping for air. Clutching his body to mine like he was my anchor for this world, an answering shiver rolled through his frame like an earthquake. His thrusts turned more erratic, and the tell-tale pulse of his high reached its peak as he came.

A low hiss seals itself against my neck, cut with little broken moans and whimpers that makes my heart swell and twist at the same time. He cleans every spare speck of blood away from the wound, and I winch slightly at the soft sting of flesh knitting itself back together. Finally Chaos stills, his hair plastered to his face with sweat and his legs trembling. My grip loosens and I let myself roll over to the side, the urge to go and clean up not quite reaching my legs at this moment. The sofa squeaks as he removes the condom and flings it far into the distance, hitting a trash can with a soggy thud. With the both of us panting for breath and eyes wide, a bolt of pure panic fires up as I hear some distant clock chime twelve times.

It was midnight.

"I have to go!" My eyes flare wide, a burst of strength rushed through my arms, and I managed to push myself up on my elbows to try and slide to the floor. A warm hand latches on to my bicep, and my head snaps around. His eyes are no longer crimson, but honey brown again. This time darkened with real fear instead of hunger.

"Stay, please?" He pleads, a quavering tremble sneaking into his voice on the last word. "Just for a little while."

I shouldn't. I really shouldn't, but the lulling weight of pure exhaustion starts to push down on my eyes. It would be so easy to just rest here for a little while. My body crumples without my control, snuggling down into his side as my eyes already start to fall shut. There is one thing I noticed though.

No one ever said how warm vampires get after drinking blood.

11

I woke up sometime later, the musty scent of old mothballs and stale air clinging to my nose, and clogged up my throat. I frowned, wriggling just the tip of my nose to try and get rid of it, but it stubbornly refused to budge. I know it wasn't time to get up already, it felt like I just fell asleep a few moments ago, but it wouldn't leave me alone. The cool weight nestled against my back pushed up slightly tighter, a lighter weight lazily draped over my hips and pulled me back against...

My eyes snapped open; the lazy contended groan pressed right into my neck wasn't nearly soft enough to stop the spike of arousal deep in my core. Or from a second pair of hips grinding a very firm cock directly against the curve of my ass. My eyes widened even further as the groan changed to something deeper, plush lips softly nibbling along my neck with just the faintest hint of sharp fangs hiding underneath. "Mmm... So warm." I flinched as he brushed against the still sensitive bite area. Even though it was healed from his magic vampire mojo, it was so sensitive that every puff of breath felt like razor blades were sliding against my skin. He responded to the sudden movement by slamming his hips directly against mine, showing off just how hard his morning wood was.

"Ahem. Missssss, I'll just leave thissssss here." A moaning voice grated out from somewhere out in the staircase. My face flushed blood red, slithering out of Chaos's grasp just as quickly as possible. Damn it! Why did Mr. Voodoo have to appear right now? Stealing the blanket that he had thrown over us sometime during the night, I padded over and grabbed the small bundle of soft silk conveniently placed just inside the door. Renea's dress. It was fixed perfectly, not the slightest sign of a tear anywhere in the violet material. A soft whine brought my attention back up to the sofa, just in time to see Chaos flip over onto his stomach with his bare ankles hanging over the side. One hand clung to the bare fabric of the couch like it was still me, small hoarse snuffles leaking out of his throat and partially muffled by the cushions

I really shouldn't sneak off like this, not after the really mind-blowing sex we had, but I had to go. Especially since I had bypassed the evening to end all evenings to try and stir up a little business. A sickening pool of dread opened up in my stomach as I could practically see those red numbers piling up right now, hear the rustling snap of the papery jaws as they gobbled up as much revenue as I could bring in.

Quickly searching and finding my discarded underwear before pushing the silky satin into place, my gaze drifted back over to Chaos in his blissfully unaware dreamland. All of the support had fallen out of his hair, the entire section tousled down into silky sapphire tipped waves that framed his eyes. One corner of his kiss swollen lips twitched up in a small smile, mine echoing the movement, and I felt guilty as all hell. I should at least give the sweet guy a note telling him how much I enjoyed spending the evening with him, and why I had to leave. A quick search of the desk produced a small notepad and pen, and I scratched out a hurried message.

Sorry I had to leave. It's nothing personal, I just had to go. The sex was awesome and you're really a sweet, caring person. I can tell. Good luck with your sister and keep up the streaming, I'll be watching. Hope you have a wonderful day, :)

Was that what you even told someone after a hookup? Have a wonderful day? Resisting the urge to slap my own head, I folded the note in half and perched it right on top of his wadded up pants. I hope it didn't flutter off. Starting towards the door, my feet stopped when he let out a small growl. It sounded like my name, and sweat started to drip down my face. I turned around, each moment stretching on for about ten years before my gaze found his. Still completely prone on the sofa, a rumbling snore leaked from his chest and gurgled in his throat. Good, he was still asleep. Growling but asleep. A sharp sigh of relief pushed out of my throat, but I had to get out of here quick or the way my heart was currently trying to ram itself out of my ribs would give me away.

My fingers brushed over the smooth metal doorknob, twisting lightly until I heard the soft click of the latch pulling back. I winched, glancing out of one eye at his body still sprawled just like he was before, and I didn't breathe again until I was up the stairs and slinking out the kitchen staff exit.

"Gooooing somewhere?" My teeth slammed down into my tongue, the bitter taste of blood quickly flooding my mouth, and I spun on my heel with my hand already clenched up tight in a fist. Of course, it sailed right through the stitched head, the bulging red eyes slowly blinking closed then open. "Heeere is yourrrr keys." The phantom butler's red stitched hand raised, and my car keys glinting dully in the center of the pale palm.

"Um… Gee. Thanks." I snatched my keys before the butler could even blink again, a light crust of ice clinging to the metal like a thin buttercream frosting. I smiled, but turned as quickly as I could and raced out of the mansion. The dark night sky was stained with the first violet rays of dawn, glowing off the sides of my slightly rusted but still perfectly usable panel truck. The dancing cake slice and spoon painted on the side of the truck smiled on towards the carefully rounded shrubs, their cheery grins looking slightly out of place against the somber iron gates looming straight ahead.

Everything was still just as I left it, even down to the veggie burger wrapper thrown onto the passenger seat from my impromptu dinner last night before I arrived at the party. Sliding in extra carefully so that I didn't damage Renea's gown any further, a quick sweep of my hand made sure that all essential parts were neatly tucked into place before I started up. With the first twist of the keys, the grumbling motor roared to life and I puttered past the gate.

Sometime later, after I had already driven a few miles down the road, it hit me like a truck. My shoes. I had left my shoes back at the Von Dracula's mansion. Oh, Renea was going to kill me. Probably skin me alive and use me for a new purse. Pulling up to a stop at a red light, my eyes flashed down to the glowing letters of the dashboard clock. 2:56 a.m. Double crap, I didn't have time to double back. Josh would be up at the cafe in about 30 minutes to get ready before the breakfast rush, and I had to unlock it for him.

The light turned green just as I glanced up in my rearview mirror, the looming figure of the Von Dracula mansion and the vampire inside faded like a crumple shadow as I drove off.

12

"Yo, Darc-Master! Can you flip the jiving steaks on a plate? My hands are full!"

"Coming" Crap! I zoned out again! Quickly swiping the back of my wrist across my forehead, my hands pulled away from the wet mound of jalapeño cheddar studded biscuit dough with a sucking pop. A few quick steps had me right at the side of the small broiler that stretched above the oven, taking just a moment to grab an oven glove before pulling the glass microwave sized door open. Three fat sandwiches of soft buttery bread were overstuffed with razor thin slices of perfectly seasoned and seared steak, topped with a thick layer of melted cheddar cheese draped over it like a blanket. The roughly chopped pepper, onion, and olive blend was Josh's own special topping, spaced between the meat and the bread for one jawbreaker of a sandwich. The warm ceramic plate tingled against my fingers, the low heat of the broiler had perfectly melted and toasted the sandwiches to perfection, and they were easy to slide right on a serving plate. Now my hands guided me down to the oven top where a pan of Josh's signature overfilled cinnamon rolls were waiting to be plucked out, one apiece landing on the plate beside each sandwich, and the chocolate cinnamon oozed filling out of each fluffy ripple. "Alright! Steak and rolls, order up!" I barked out, shoving the plate up into the window.

"Thank you," Meadow trilled, her long rainbow-colored braids swaying with the movement as she tossed a wink my way. Quickly whisking the plate away on its journey to a hungry customer, the empty space was replaced by a second and then a third as I tried to catch up with the plates that Josh was slinging out like a racing event.

"So, did you have fun last night at the fancy party?" Expertly using one hand to flip over a fluffy potato bun toasting on the griddle, and the other to slide a rapidly browning veggie burger patty onto the opposite side. Josh tossed a curious glance over his broad shoulder, his green and blue eyes twinkling with a teasing sparkle that brought a guilty blush straight up to my cheeks.

"It was fine." Crap! Surely he couldn't tell what really happened last night. My stomach jumped clear up into my throat, making my eyes water, and I quickly shook my head and reached for the next plate. My eyes flashed up, catching the next ticket order as it flashed across the display screen perched high on the wall. A single slice of raspberry chocolate pie, no problem. I reached for a knife and a pie server, the chocolate crust and creamy blush pink filling parting easily with two swipes. I'd have to get back to my dough in just a moment, or the entire batch of biscuits would be ruined.

"Aw, come on! You got to party with Crescent City's best! There's got to be a heck of a story- Crap!" The crack and sizzle of flames bursting into life made me spin, my fingers almost letting go of the knife in pure shock. A dancing blaze of orange flames had engulfed the part of the griddle where the bun was, quickly charring the soft brown edges into a crusty coal black. Josh's swears switched to something lower, his eyes closing as he laid one hand on the griddle's controls, and started chanting in a different language. The blaze immediately died down into nothing, the entire surface cooling down as magic worked where mortal means couldn't reach. At least his magic was working together today and not randomly exploding things.

"Darcy!" Renea's undeniable voice screeched out. "You gotta see this!"

Letting my head hang down, I pinched my forefinger and thumb across the bridge of my nose, trying to stave off the migraine that was threatening to pound my skull into little walnut shells. "In here!" She should have known that already considering how busy we were this morning.

The thud-thud-thud of her crutches hitting the floor sounded like a bass drum, the dirge like countdown to my doom. Filled with nervous energy, my hands shifted into autopilot and started filling the orders all on their own. A Cluckin' Chicken sandwich, Autumn Squash soup, and a snack pack of a Cream Cheese muffin and house made Granola all assembled in just a few minutes, passing on out the window. I had just made my way back to my dough when the kitchen doors nearly swung off their hinges, and my heart sank to my knees as my doom approached.

"Ohmygawd! Did you see! We're on the front page!" With this morning's newspaper tightly clasped between her crutch and her left arm, Renea clunked into the kitchen with the brightest beauty pageant smile I've ever seen. The shimmering gold sequined mini dress couldn't hold a light to her sparkling eyes, and I had to resist cupping one hand over my eyes just to dim the glow. "Look, look, look!"

Slowly wiping my hands on my flour encrusted apron until my skin was starting to turn red, the ever-deepening pit in my stomach felt like it could swallow me whole right now. But she sounded way too happy for it to be anything bad. Surely it wasn't a total load of crap taking up the front page. Reluctantly raising my eyes, I held my breath as my gaze slowly wandered across the inked words.

"" The Name Your Slice Cafe and Bakery saved the Von Dracula's Birthday Gala!" A source close to Crescent City's most illustrious family said after a surprising series of events left the event in need of a new caterer, and our city's skilled chefs at the Name Your Slice Cafe stepped up to the plate. A complete hit with their fabulous Triple Layer Chocolate Cherry Blood Cake, the Von Dracula family sincerely thanks the entire staff at Name Your Slice for their last-minute efforts to make their Gala a success. It's their overwhelming advice that anyone who needs a top-level caterer for their event to contact the business as soon as possible." Josh read what my tongue refused to. One eyebrow arched high in surprise, nearly brushing his hairline in pure shock. "Darc, you know what this means, right?"

"This means that we're gonna rule this town forever!" Tossing her crutches aside, Renea lunged for Josh in a full body tackle, complete with a blood curdling squeal that froze my hands in midair. The taller man easily caught her with one arm, cackling with pure delight as the two of them spun around in the center of the kitchen like they weren't surrounded by hundreds of dangerous objects.

As for me, I just stood there completely numb. Like numb as in I couldn't feel anything below my neck, but my mind was churning overtime. Had they really liked my cake that much? It was almost too good to be true. A recommendation like that didn't usually come that easy, not unless there were some heavy strings still attached. What was even weirder was that I never spoke with anyone in the Von Dracula family.

The kitchen doors burst open again, revealing Axe's swollen face rounded the corner as he glared at the twirling duo. "Damn, you two are loud. Turn it down, will ya?" His slightly lopsided brilliant gaze shifted to mine, the wolf gold glow instantly freezing any spare blood in my veins into ice. "Darcy, there's two people standing out front. They want to speak with you, *alone.*" The last word came out as a threatening growl, a shudder rippling through his sturdy frame like he was just seconds away from going full wolf right here in the kitchen.

"Thanks, Axe. How's your eye?" I said, trying to convince myself that even if he was half feral, he surely had enough self-preservation skills not to go psycho in my kitchen.

"It's fine. Just a leftover from last night's gig." He sniffed, deliberately avoiding my gaze to glare his spine melting best at Renea and Josh. I couldn't even begin to guess what had happened last night in his PI work to give him such a horrible black eye, the entire area around his left eye was swollen up from eyebrow to cheekbone, and stained a glossy cherry red that was in the process of darkening to a deep plum. Only a sliver of eye could actually be seen on that side, and I lightly patted his thick shoulder as I slipped past. He didn't reply again, not even when I yanked my flour caked apron over my head and tossed it onto the nearest counter. Giving myself a quick fluff for any stray crumbs, it gave me the half a moment of thought I needed to actually process what had happened so far today. A line twelve deep was standing outside the café door at opening time this morning, and it had only gotten busier from there. We were running all hands on deck, even using Josh's questionable magic despite it being a big no-no from the state board. I hope whoever it was, it wasn't anyone with a camera, or they were going to be very disappointed that being a cafe owner isn't as glamorous as some would think.

Steeling myself for an irate customer, or maybe someone who just needed a special order. I stepped past the swinging doors and up behind the counter where Meadow was ringing up a set of customers at the cash register. "Thank you so much!" She trilled, passing over the change to the taller of the two and stepped aside, letting in a full view of the two customers standing there in waiting.

I gasped, stopping dead in mid stride like someone had just punched my off button.

"Hello there! You must be the special chef lady that my son spoke of." With a shock of thick grey hair carefully curved back, the top of the older gentleman's light grey eyes barely reached over the top of the counter. He smiled, showing off the sharp fanged teeth that had inspired more than a few tales of his long life, but they also left out a few things. Count Von Dracula was not the tall handsome monster featured in so much Hollywood media, but a slightly shrunken older man sank deep into a black wheelchair. The brilliant cotton candy blue and papaya orange tropical shirt shook off any of that cape nonsense, and his weathered skin looked a shade darker than old tanned leather. Apparently, the Count had a frequent love for the sun. "He didn't mention that you were so beautiful." The thick black caterpillar-like brows knit together in a scowl, one age spotted hand reaching across the counter to shake my hand. "I suppose he was trying to keep that for himself, but I wanted to thank you in person for such wonderful service."

"Dad! Don't be creepy!" Son? My gaze raised to the second member of the duo who stood just behind the Count. Anxiously shuffling from foot to foot, Chaos barely glanced me in the eye before his gaze dropped down to his feet. His cheeks had flushed so red that it looked like all his blood was contained in just that spot, and his hands had shoved deep into the stomach pockets of his oversized black hoodie that it threatened to tear. His hair had been swept back up into a slightly puffed swoop, one that let the sunlight streaming through the windows play off the golden undertones of his skin, and the sapphire scales of his dragon tattoo. "Sorry about that. Dad means well, he just... well. Doesn't get how some things sound off." His plush lips twisted up into a shy smile, the deep honey of his eyes glowing so warmly that it took a moment for my brain to remember to breathe.

"It's not a problem. Glad you enjoyed it." Sticking my hand out, the Count vigorously squeezed so hard that my bones cracked, and shook so quickly that I thought my shoulder would pop right out of my socket. Ouch! Something like a smile was painted across my lips, but it felt like a tight grimace, and I was counting each second until he let it drop.

"Oh, I certainly did. My daughter never lets me have sweets anymore, but even she couldn't keep me out of that wonderful cake." A sly glint crept up in his eyes, changing the watery amber a shade darker. A flash of sapphire blue caught the edge of my vision, and my gaze dropped for about half a second, but it was more than enough to see the same sapphire dragon tattoo wound tight around his left forearm. "If your baking skills are any indication of your personality, we're going to get along just fine while we work together. Ms. Blanchard."

I think my jaw dropped to the floor, but it was so numb that I couldn't really feel it. A few garbled mumbles drifted off my tongue, but the Count merely laughed and waved it off without a care. Working together, as in the future? He wanted to work together again? A second round of whooped screeches echoed from the kitchen, Renea and Josh's mostly with a few rumbling growls from Axe mixed in. This was a dream come true!

"Hey, Dad." Chaos's soft voice pulled me slightly out of the daze, the sharp crinkling of something paper-like drew my gaze over to where he was bending down to pick something up off the floor. A small square bag, decorated completely in pink glitter and with matching fuzzy feather boa handles, looked completely out of place against the cackling skull and crossbones decorating the chest of his hoodie. "You mind giving us a minute?" He arched one brow high, jingling the bag slightly so that I could hear the contents rattle inside.

The Count chuckled warmly, "Don't mind me. I'll just be over here saying hello to this little hunka hunka burning love over there." Dropping his hands down to the wheels, he rolled off in the direction of a deuce table of two grey haired ladies sharing an order of crispy seasoned fries. They immediately started beaming as soon as his wheels reached their table, anxiously patting their perfectly coiffed hair with one hand while he proceeded to kiss the bridge of their knuckles on the other.

"Big Sis is going to kill me if Dad charms another old lady into marriage." Chaos's soft voice drifted on a whisper, and I tilted my head slightly to the side as he scowled in their direction.

"You're a Von Dracula?" My eyes widened as soon as my tongue blurted it out. Crap! My hand clapped over my lips, but it was too late. Chaos just chuckled slightly, placing his gift bag up on the counter, and flashed one of those spine melting gazes that left me weak in the knees. "Were you behind the article in the paper this morning?"

"Yep, and yes! I'm the baby boy. My real name is Sebastian. Sebastian Von Dracula, at your service." Twisting his arm over his stomach, he tipped forward in a small bow, and my arms flew out to try and catch his forehead before it met the sharp edge of the slate countertop. I wasn't fast enough. His forehead dully thudded against the hard surface, one of my eyes closing in sympathy, but he bounced right back up like a little rubber ball.

Well... a grimacing rubber ball that is. "I hope you're not mad, but I really want Dad to meet you after your cake was such a hit last night. And I wanted to give this to you. It's something you forgot during our... *encounter* last night."

With a small nudge, he pushed the feathery bag my way, and flashed another one of those shy grins. I swallowed heavily, half dreading what might be inside, but I reached out and pulled the bag closer. My hands were shaking, the fluffy paper crackling like a rattlesnake's rattle as my fingers wove through it. Then the tips brushed against something familiar, something very soft and very high. A little murmur of surprise left my lips as I pushed the paper away to see Renea's six-inch black velvet heels carefully nestled into a nest of tissue paper. "My shoes! How did you know?"

"It was a lucky guess." His gaze dropped to the floor like it was magnetic, a bright red flush lighting up his cheeks again as he started shuffling his combat boot clad feet against one another. "After I found your note and your shoes, I wanted to get them back to you. That's when Dad started raving about your cake, and I remembered that you said that you baked it, and I thought your name and address would be in my sister's files. I didn't tell Dad about what happened between us, but when he found out that I was coming to see you, he wouldn't let me leave without him coming along." Chaos was out of breath by the time he finished, each word pouring out like a little mini geyser erupting from his throat.

"Thanks a lot, I really appreciate it." That lame statement couldn't even begin to cover what I felt. Piece by piece, the guilty weight slipped free from my shoulders as my mind slowly processed the fact that the Count loved my cake, and that he had loved it so much that he gave a five star review to the newspaper. With the lack of anything else to do, my fingers idly plucked at the handles of the bag, sending small scraps of pink feathers fluttering over the counter. "Thanks to you and your family, I'll have enough business to keep my café running for fifty years or more."

"I'm glad we could help." Subtly glancing left and right to make sure we weren't attracting any extra attention, I could feel the prickle of four sets of eyes against my back, and I had to push down the urge to scream at my friends to quit gawking and get back to work. If he could sense their attention, Chaos didn't let on. Instead, he leaned forward. Resting his folded arms directly onto the counter, we were almost nose to nose and my fingers curled under against my palms. "There is something I wanted to ask you." He blinked slowly, the silky fringe of dark lashes fanning like butterfly wings against his cheeks. My breath hitched, a hot spark lighting up my veins until they simmered beneath my skin, and I tipped my head for him to continue. "I'd really like to see you again. If you would like, and we can get to know each other properly. Maybe you could even teach me some of your grandmother's baking skills, but I really like to get to know the lady behind this awesome business. What you like, don't like, and all that stuff. I hope that doesn't sound as dumb as it did in my head."

I smiled so hard that my cheeks hurt. "Don't worry, it's not dumb at all. I'd really like that a lot." Reaching out, my fingers quickly wove through his own and held tight. When our palms touched, the sparks flared once again but they were more the comforting type instead of so much wildfire. He answered my smile with one of his own, and even though it was so cold the windows had frosted over, I had never been warmer.

Now I couldn't wait to see what the future held.

Don't miss out!

Visit the website below and you can sign up to receive emails whenever Clair Gardenwell publishes a new book. There's no charge and no obligation.

https://books2read.com/r/B-A-KGFK-BBOPB

BOOKS 2 READ

Connecting independent readers to independent writers.

Did you love *One Night With A Vampire*? Then you should read *Foxgloves Are For Deception*[1] by Clair Gardenwell!

[2]

Magic always has a price.

The legendary kingdom of Lyquirz. A kingdom of life, magic, and death. Ruled by a queen with an iron hand so stiff that no one even dares speak her name, the people hide their magic lest they be recruited into an army and forced to fight in a battle that leads only to death.

But there is one.

Regina Laelia, a girl cursed by birth, an herbalist in training, and the kingdom's only hope. Her magic is the darkest kind,

---

1. https://books2read.com/u/3yeOdZ

2. https://books2read.com/u/3yeOdZ

shadow magic, capable of manipulating people against their will. Day and night, she hides her magic to avoid detection, but fate can't be avoided for long. Destruction, fire, and death throws her into a desperate race for survival, one that she has to win at all costs.

She's not alone.

Joined by her childhood friend turned doctor with an insatiable flirty attitude for the ladies, a blind ex-knight who seems determined to protect her at every turn despite his hatred for magic, and a baby dragon that can't stand her in the least. She has to learn that sometimes you have to be a little bad to be good, and that her past and her future is more mysterious than she knows.

Read more at https://books2read.com/ap/nzz5Vm/Clair-Gardenwell.

About the Author

A life long lover of reading, Clair is a classic introvert that loves animals, a cool glass of lemonade, and a a thick book on her lap. She is always on the hunt for an idea for her next novel, her inspiration frequently coming after a nap or a binge of her favorite shows.

You can find her at the following sites for all the latest news.

Twitter: @happybookowl or Clair Gardenwell

Facebook: @happybookowl or Clair Gardenwell

Read more at https://books2read.com/ap/nzz5Vm/ Clair-Gardenwell.

www.ingramcontent.com/pod-product-compliance
Lightning Source LLC
Chambersburg PA
CBHW071228130726
47998CB00002B/870